W9-BMT-624

For Patacake Nursery—T. M.
For Henry and Horace—A. P.

The Publisher thanks the British Airways Community Learning Center at
Heathrow Airport in London, England, for their kind assistance in the development of this book.

KINGFISHER
LONDON & NEW YORK

Text copyright © 2002 by Tony Mitton
Illustrations © 2002 by Ant Parker
Cover design by Perfect Bound Ltd

Published 2017 by Kingfisher,
Published in the United States by Kingfisher,
175 Fifth Ave., New York, NY 10010
Kingfisher is an imprint of Macmillan Children's Books, London.
All rights reserved.

Distributed in the U.S. and Canada by Macmillan,
175 Fifth Ave., New York, NY 10010

Kingfisher books are available for special promotions and premiums.
For details contact: Special Markets Department, Macmillan,
175 Fifth Avenue, New York, NY 10010.

For more information, please visit www.kingfisherbooks.com

Library of Congress Cataloging-in-Publication Data
has been applied for

ISBN: 978-0-7534-7328-3

Printed in China
9 8 7 6 5 4 3 2 1
1TR/0417/UG/LEO/128MA

AMAZING AIRPLANES
SOUND BOOK

Tony Mitton and

Ant Parker

Whoosh

Sun cream

KINGFISHER
LONDON & NEW YORK

Whoosh

An airplane is amazing,
for it travels through the sky,

Press here to hear an amazing sound!

above the clouds for miles and miles,
so very fast and high!

An airport is the place you go
to take a trip by air.

You check in at the terminal
to show you've paid your fare.

The ground crew weighs your baggage
and loads it in the hold.

And then you take the walkway
to the plane when you are told.

The flight deck's where the captain
and copilot do their jobs.
They both know how to fly the plane
with all its dials and knobs.

They radio Control Tower to check
the runway's clear.
They can't take off unless it is,
with other planes so near.

By intercom the captain on the flight deck
says hello.

You have to put your seat belt on
before the plane can go!

A plane is big and heavy,
yet it climbs up really high.

It zooms along the runway
and soars into the sky.

Whoosh

Its wings hold big jet engines,
which are loud and very strong.
They suck in air and blow it through
to whoosh the plane along.

When the plane moves fast enough,
the air around's so swift
it pushes up beneath the wings
and makes the whole plane lift.

Soon the plane is in the air,
so now you're on your flight.
The cabin crew look after you
and make sure you're all right.

They bring you drinks and magazines
and trays of food to eat.
And sometimes there's a movie
you can watch while in your seat.

When the journey's over,
the captain lands the plane.
Control Tower has to say it's safe
for coming down again.

You sit with seat belt fastened,
there's a bumpy, rumbling sound—
the wheels are making contact,
and the plane is on the ground!

At last the doors are opening.
Then out you come with smiles.

So give a cheer. Hooray—you're here!
You've flown for miles and miles.

Collect all the **AMAZING MACHINES** books by Tony Mitton and Ant Parker!

HC ISBN 978-0-7534-5403-9
TP ISBN 978-0-7534-5915-7

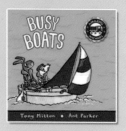

TP ISBN 978-0-7534-5916-4

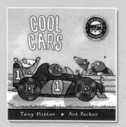

HC ISBN 978-0-7534-5802-0
TP ISBN 978-0-7534-7207-1

TP ISBN 978-0-7534-5304-9

TP ISBN 978-0-7534-5307-0

HC ISBN 978-0-7534-7290-3
TP ISBN 978-0-7534-7291-0

HC ISBN 978-0-7534-7292-7
TP ISBN 978-0-7534-7293-4

TP ISBN 978-0-7534-5305-6

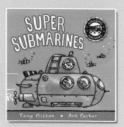

TP ISBN 978-0-7534-7208-8

TP ISBN 978-0-7534-5306-3

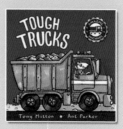

TP ISBN 978-0-7534-5917-1

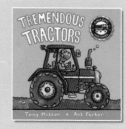

TP ISBN 978-0-7534-5918-8

Younger children will love these **AMAZING MACHINES** board books:

ISBN 978-0-7534-7233-0

ISBN 978-0-7534-7231-6

ISBN 978-0-7534-7234-7

ISBN 978-0-7534-7232-3

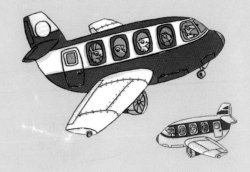

Get busy with the **AMAZING MACHINES** activity books—with a model to make and stickers!

ISBN 978-0-7534-7255-2

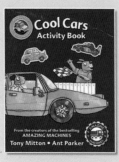

ISBN 978-0-7534-7296-5

ISBN 978-0-7534-7256-9

ISBN 978-0-7534-7257-6

ISBN 978-0-7534-7295-8

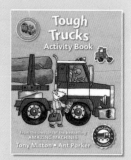

ISBN 978-0-7534-7254-5